A Tale of
TWO SEDERS

In memory of my Themper aunts, Dorothy, Ida, and
Pauline; cousins Barbara Johnson and Elaine Roswig;
and great-uncle Louis Shapiro, who made my childhood
seders sweet. – M.A.P.

To Sebastián, and only to him – V.C.

Text copyright © 2010 by Mindy Avra Portnoy
Illustrations copyright © 2010 by Lerner Publishing Group

Kar-Ben Publishing
A division of Lerner Publishing Group, Inc.
241 First Avenue North
Minneapolis, MN 55401 U.S.A
1-800-4KARBEN

www.karben.com

Library of Congress Cataloging-in-Publication Data

Portnoy, Mindy Avra.
    A tale of two Seders / by Mindy Avra Portnoy ; illustrated by Valeria Cis.
        p.   cm.
    Summary: After her parents' divorce, a young girl experiences a variety of Passover seders.
        Includes recipes and facts about Passover.
    ISBN: 978-0-8225-9907-4 (lib. bdg. : alk. paper)
        [1. Seder—Fiction. 2. Passover—Fiction. 3. Judaism—Customs and practices—Fiction.
    4. Divorce—Fiction. 5. Family life—Fiction.] I. Cis, Valeria, ill. II. Title.
    PZ7.P8375Tal 2010
    [E]—dc22   2008033570

Manufactured in the United States of America
1—BP—12/15/09

A Tale of
TWO SEDERS

By Mindy Avra Portnoy   Illustrated by Valeria Cis

KAR-BEN
PUBLISHING

The year after my mom and dad stopped being married to each other, I went to two seders in two places— one at Dad's apartment, and one at Mom's house.

Luckily, like many Jewish families, we have two seders, which makes Passover a lot easier than Thanksgiving, when there's also lots of food, but you have to decide where to eat it.

I have my own room in each place. The one at Mom's has blue-flowered wallpaper and a fish tank. My room at Dad's is painted yellow and has a doggie bed for Ollie, our beagle.

I keep some clothes and DVDs and books in both places, so I don't have to remember to bring everything with me when I move back and forth. Both Mom and Dad keep my favorite foods, though Dad sometimes forgets to buy chocolate milk, and Mom won't let me eat Fruit Loops.

Mom and Dad were divorced three years ago,
so since then I've been to six different seders.

The first year when I had just turned seven, Dad invited his friends Gabe and Lisa, who brought me a coloring book about Passover and a brand new box of crayons. They kept smiling and being nice to me. I think they were worried that I wouldn't have a good time without my mom. I sang The Four Questions all the way through in Hebrew. Grandpa Stan told his usual silly jokes, and Ollie barked all the way through Dayenu. Dad's charoset didn't really stick together, but his matzah balls sure did, maybe a little too much!

MATZAH

The next night, Mom invited her friends Laura, Ruth, and Samantha to the seder. They told stories about Moses's sister Miriam, who led the Israelites in celebration after they crossed the sea to freedom. Auntie Evelyn brought along her guitar, and we danced around the table. Everyone drank more than four cups of wine—except me.

I could tell Mom was still a little sad, because she didn't eat very much. The seder went on forever, and I fell asleep before it was over. Mom's charoset was very sticky and tasted mostly like figs.

The next year, there were eight of us at Mom's seder
the first night, including two guys she knew from work.
We used a new Haggadah with lots of pictures and stories. Auntie
Evelyn made some very sweet charoset from a Yemenite recipe.
I asked Mom where Yemen was. She told me it was in Southern
Arabia, and that many Jews from Yemen were airlifted to Israel
in Operation Magic Carpet. That night I dreamed that my dad
flew back to our old house on a magic carpet.

The second night, Dad brought his new friend Gail to the seder. She gave me a whole box of chocolate lollipops. Gabe and Lisa brought their new baby Zach, who cried the whole time I was singing The Four Questions.

Grandpa Stan fell asleep and began to snore. In the morning, Dad cooked fried matzah for me, and asked if I liked Gail. I wasn't sure, but the lollipops were terrific.

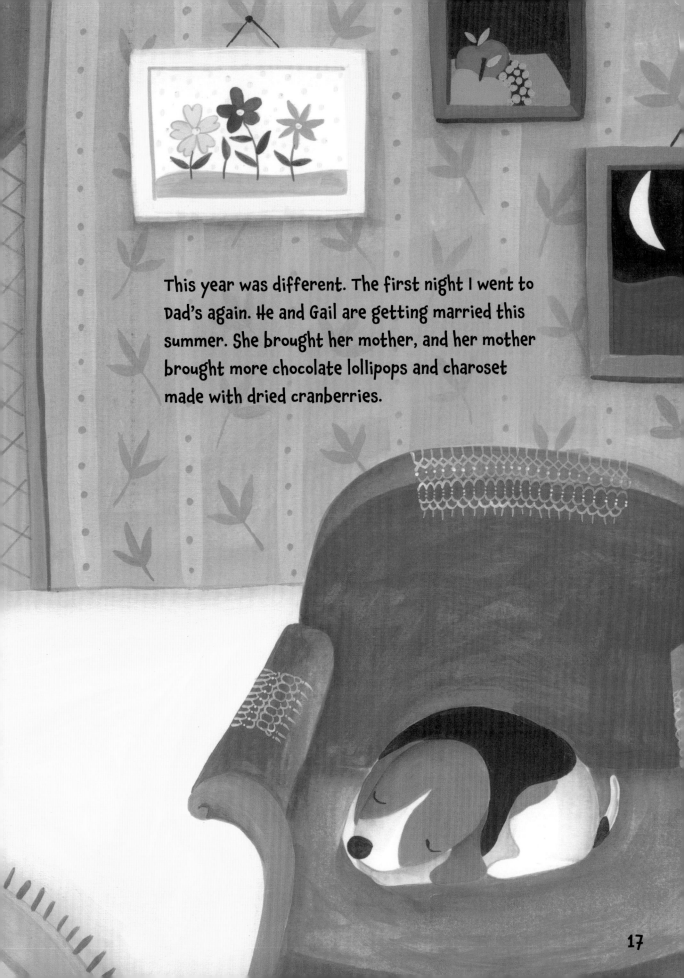

This year was different. The first night I went to Dad's again. He and Gail are getting married this summer. She brought her mother, and her mother brought more chocolate lollipops and charoset made with dried cranberries.

When I sang The Four Questions, baby Zach clapped. But I was sad that Grandpa Stan wasn't there to hear me. He's in the hospital getting a new knee, but Dad says he'll be home soon. I missed his jokes and songs and even his snoring. Gail's mom said I could call her "Grandma" if I want to, but I'll have to think about that.

That night, I dreamed that my whole family was back together in our old house. Mom and Dad were leading the seder, Gabe and Lisa were there along with Grandpa Stan and Auntie Evelyn. The charoset was perfect—figs and dates and wine and apples and nuts all together in the right mix. We sang and danced and laughed.

But when I woke up, I was still in Dad's apartment.

On the second night, Mom promised a surprise. She had decided we would go to the Temple for seder, since several of her friends were visiting family, and Auntie Evelyn was taking a Passover cruise. I wondered what kind of charoset they have on a cruise ship.

When we arrived at the Temple, my best friend Katie was standing near the door. We had never been to a seder together, so we were excited! But as I entered the social hall, I saw more people I knew—Gail and her mother, and Dad! What were they doing here? Didn't they know Mom and I were coming? Dad came up and gave me a hug and said hi to Mom. They told me that they'd decided it would be nice for all of us to be together for one night of the holiday.

23

The seder was noisy and it was hard to hear the little kids ask The Four Questions. The charoset was okay but not as good as homemade.

Katie and I got prizes for finding the afikomen!

So my dream had come true—well, almost. The next day,
Dad took me to see Grandpa Stan in the hospital. I brought
him a chocolate lollipop.

28

That night when Mom tucked me in, she told me that families are like charoset. Some have more ingredients than others, some stick together better than others, some are sweeter than others. But each one is tasty in its own way.

CHAROSET RECIPES

Yemenite Charoset

½ c. almonds, chopped
½ c. dried apricots, chopped
8 dried figs, chopped
2 tsp. ground coriander
2 tsp grated rind of lime
    or lemon

1 Tbsp. honey
¼ c. sweet white wine
2 Tbsp. toasted sesame
    seeds*

Combine all ingredients and refrigerate for one hour. Form into one-inch balls and roll in sesame seeds.
Makes about 24 balls.

Ashkenazim do not eat sesame seeds on Passover, so you may want to substitute ground nuts.

Israeli Charoset

1 apple, peeled and quartered
3 bananas, sliced
10 pitted dates
¼ c. almonds
¼ c. walnuts
Juice and grated rind
    of ½ lemon

Juice and grated rind
    of ½ orange
½ c. sweet red wine
1 tsp. cinnamon
1 Tbsp. honey
5 Tbsp. matzah meal

Combine in food processor or chop until blended. Makes 2-3 cups.

Traditional Ashkenazi Charoset

1 c. apples, chopped
1 c. walnuts, chopped

1 tsp. cinnamon
1 Tbsp. sweet red wine

Combine all ingredients in food processor or chop until blended.
Makes 1½ cup.

CHAIroset

This 18-ingredient charoset is an Italian tradition. The Hebrew letters in the word Chai (chet and yod) which mean life, have a numerical equivalent of 18.

1 c. apricots
3 apples, peeled and cubed
2 bananas, peeled and sliced
1 lemon, juice and rind
1 orange, peeled and
    sectioned
1 c. walnuts or pecans
1 c. cashews
1 c. pitted prunes
1 c. pitted dates

1 c. dried figs
2 tsp. cinnamon
½ c. almonds
½ c. hazelnuts
Dash nutmeg
Dash mace or cloves
Dash coriander
¼ c. matzah meal
½ c. sweet wine

Combine in large bowl and mix well. Add to food processer in batches and process until chunky. Add additional wine to moisten if necessary.
Makes about 2 quarts.

Courtesy Loretta Vitale Saks

GLOSSARY

Afikomen — the special piece of matzah hidden at the seder to keep children involved

Charoset — a mixture of apples, nuts, cinnamon, and wine (and sometimes figs, dates, and other fruits) representing the mortar used by the Jewish slaves in building cities for the Egyptian Pharaoh

Dayenu — the Hebrew word for "It would have been enough for us," a song of gratitude sung at the seder

Four Cups of Wine — Jews traditionally drink four cups of wine at the seder to recall God's four promises of redemption to the Israelite slaves

Four Questions — traditionally asked by the youngest at the seder, the Questions pertain to the unusual seder foods and rituals

Haggadah — literally meaning "to tell," the special book of prayers, psalms, rituals, and text read at the seder

Matzah — unleavened bread

Operation Magic Carpet — the secret airlift of 45,000 Yemenite Jews to the new state of Israel in 1949-50

Passover — Jewish holiday that commemorates the biblical story of the exodus from Egypt

Seder — the Hebrew word for "order," the word for the communal meal at which the story of the Exodus is retold and ritual foods are eaten

ABOUT THE AUTHOR

Mindy Avra Portnoy is the author of four previous books, including *Where Do People Go When They Die?* and *Matzah Ball: A Passover Story* (Kar-Ben). She is a graduate of Yale University and was ordained at the Hebrew Union College-Jewish Institute of Religion. She is the Rabbi of Temple Sinai in Washington, D.C.

ABOUT THE ILLUSTRATOR

Valeria Cis was born and raised in the city of Rosario, Argentina, where she still lives with her little son, Facundo, and her husband, Sebastián. Valeria studied fine art at The University of Humanities and Arts in Rosario. When not illustrating, she likes to spend her time playing with her son and collecting wooden chairs and old irons.